T0193471

BEFORE I MEET MOMMY AND DADDY 2

Written By
Avery L Rogers.Sr

Illustrated By
Ishika Sharma

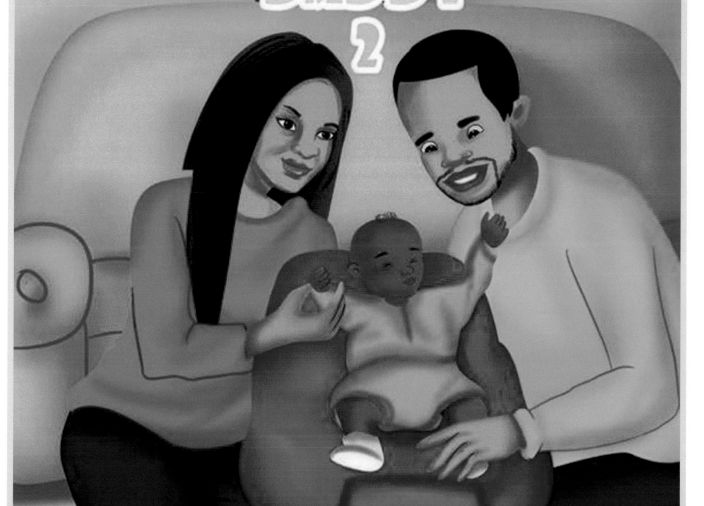

Copyright © 2021 by Avery L Rogers Sr. 828596

All rights reserved. No part of this book may be
reproduced or transmitted in any form or by any
means, electronic or mechanical, including photocopying,
recording, or by any information storage and retrieval
system, without permission in writing from the copyright
owner.

This is a work of fiction. Names, characters, places
and incidents either are the product of the author's
imagination or are used fictitiously, and any resemblance
to any actual persons, living or dead, events, or locales is
entirely coincidental.

To order additional copies of this book, contact:
Xlibris
844-714-8691
www.Xlibris.com
Orders@Xlibris.com

ISBN: 978-1-6641-6609-7 (sc)
ISBN: 978-1-6641-6610-3 (hc)
ISBN: 978-1-6641-6608-0 (e)

Print information available on the last page

Rev. date: 03/30/2021

Wow, there they are! My parents, the people that created me. I've heard Mommy and Daddy but now I can see them too. My parents! Now it's time, for what they have planned for me., Yayyy! I'm so excited!

It's time for me to see my new home,
and my new bed... my old one was water.
Mommy and me are ready to go now.

Daddy puts me in what's called a car seat. It is really cool, it has space shields and belt's and other cool stuff hanging from it. Weeeee!

12 months later ....

Today's my Big Day! My birthday! I pretend
to be sleeping as Mommy and Daddy
bust in singing Happy Birthday. Then they
announce.... "We're going to Disneyland!"

My first birthday is a huge Adventure, and it starts at Disneyland; that's where I discover I want to be a kid forever. Eating ice cream, cotton candy, giving hugs and hi-fives. Goldennnnn! I secretly hear Mommy and Daddy secretly planning my birthday party, but they need ideas.

Off to the Magical Spaceship. It takes us under the sea for the Sea World Adventure! We see a group of sharks celebrating a new baby shark's birthday., As we continue through the sea, we notice a big party. While the baby looks on in amazement, Mommy and Daddy at that moment have a great idea for the baby's party.

Mommy's idea is to have a backyard Water Exhibit with all the animals we had seen during our Sea World adventure.

But there is a problem --, we don't have a backyard; but Mommy and Daddy have a plan and super powers. I am told to close my eyes and count to three. And then I open my eyes.

There are all my friends and sea friends!
We have all our scuba gear on. I give
Mommy and Daddy the biggest hug ever.
We all play games and sing for hours.

As we continue to play, Mommy calls my name...
As I wake up, I notice a puddle of water from my
dream adventure..., and I began to tell Mommy
and Daddy about the amazing dream I just had.

To Be Continued...

To Be Continued...

Printed in the United States
by Baker & Taylor Publisher Services